NABEEL'S NEW PANTS

An Eid Tale

retold by
Fawzia Gilani-Williams
illustrations by
Proiti Roy

Marshall Cavendish Children

Glossary

Abbu (ab-BOO): father.

Amma (am-MAH): mother.

Asalaamu alaikum (a-SA-laamu a-LAY-kum): a common greeting among Muslims, meaning "Peace be with you."

Biryani (bir-EE-ah-NEE): a dish made from rice, spices, meat, and/or vegetables.

Burqa (BUR-kah): an outer garment with a veil worn by some Muslim women.

Dupatta (DOO-paht-uh): a long scarf draped over the shoulders or over the head.

Eid (eed): a holiday that marks the end of Ramadan, the Islamic holy month of fasting.

Mosque (mosk): a place of worship for Muslims.

Samosa (sa-MOH-sah): a pastry shell filled with a mixture of spiced potatoes, onion, peas and cilantro; minced meat; or fresh paneer (a type of cheese).

Sheerkorma (shir-KOR-mah): a sweet made with vermicelli (a kind of pasta), coconut, and dried fruit.

Wa alaikum salaam (wa-Lay-kum sa-LAM): a common response to the greeting "Asalaamu alaikum," meaning "And upon you be peace."

With God's permission, to my loving parents, Munir and Shabbir; Judy and Terry. And to my Robert and my Muslimah. With love and peace to the world.
—F.G-W.

To my daughter, Shoi
—P.R.

Copyright © 2007 by Tulika Publishers
First Marshall Cavendish edition, 2010
Originally published by Tulika Publishing, Chennai, India, 2007

All rights reserved
Marshall Cavendish Corporation
99 White Plains Road
Tarrytown, NY 10591
www.marshallcavendish.us/kids

The illustrations are rendered in Indian ink
and gouache water-based paint.
Book design by Vera Soki
Editor: Nathalie Le Du

Printed in China (E)
1 3 5 6 4 2

 **Marshall Cavendish** Children

Library of Congress Cataloging-in-Publication Data

Gilani, Fawzia.
  [Ismat's Eid]
  Nabeel's new pants : an Eid tale / by Fawzia Gilani-Williams;
illustrations by Proiti Roy. — 1st Marshall Cavendish ed.
     p. cm.
  Summary: While buying gifts for his family to wear to the
mosque on Eid a shoemaker is persuaded to get new pants
for himself, but the only pair available is too long and no one
seems to have time to shorten them.
  ISBN 978-0-7614-5629-2
  [1. Pants—Fiction. 2. Muslims—Fiction. 3. Family life—
Turkey—Fiction.
4. Turkey—Fiction.] I. Roy, Proiti, ill. II. Title.
PZ7.G372Nab 2010
  [E]—dc22   2009024001

Nabeel the shoemaker

had been very busy. Tomorrow was *Eid*. All day, people had been trying out new shoes and now they were all sold out.

"Ah!" sighed Nabeel. "At last I can go and buy some gifts for my family." He closed his little shoe stall and walked down to the clothes shop.

"*Asalaamu alaikum*, Hamza," Nabeel greeted the shopkeeper. "I want to buy my wife a *burqa* for *Eid*!"

"*Wa alaikum salaam*," replied Hamza. "I have just the one for her."

"And perhaps a *dupatta* for my mother?" asked Nabeel.

Hamza's Shop

"How about this one?" said Hamza, pulling out a bright blue cloth embroidered with tiny beads.

"And some bangles for my daughter."

Hamza showed Nabeel hundreds of bangles. It was very hard to choose, they were all so pretty.

Nabeel was pleased with the gifts. He paid Hamza and turned to leave.

"Wait," called Hamza. "What about you? Your pants are full of patches. Why don't you buy yourself a new pair?"

"Ah, perhaps I will," said Nabeel.

But when they looked, they found only one pair of pants. Nabeel held them up to his waist. "Four fingers too long," he said. He pulled on his beard and then looked up at Hamza with a smile. "Could you shorten them for me, please?"

"I'm so sorry," replied Hamza. "Not today. I have to get ready for *Eid*. Why don't you ask your wife?"

"That's a good idea." Nabeel nodded and hurried home.

"This is beautiful!" exclaimed Yasmeen, when she saw the *burqa*. "I love the color. I will wear it for *Eid*!" Then she looked at Nabeel and said, "Did you get anything for yourself?"

"Yes," said Nabeel, "a pair of pants."

Yasmeen held up the pants and frowned. "These are four fingers too long," she said.

"Yes," said Nabeel. "Could you shorten them for me?"

"Not today," she replied. "I have no time. Tomorrow is *Eid*, and I have to make *biryani*. Why don't you ask your mother?"

Habiba's
House

Nabeel went to see his mother, Habiba.

"*Amma*, I have brought you a gift," he said and pulled out the bright blue *dupatta*.

"This is beautiful!" exclaimed Habiba. "I love the color. I will wear it for *Eid*!" Then she looked at Nabeel and said, "Did you get anything for yourself?"

"Yes," said Nabeel, "a pair of pants."

Habiba held up the pants and frowned. "These are four fingers too long," she said.

"Yes," said Nabeel. "Could you shorten them for me?"

"Not today," said his mother. "I have no time. Tomorrow is *Eid*, and I have to make *sheerkorma*. Why don't you ask Mariam?"

Nabeel went to see his daughter. "Mariam, I have brought you a gift," said Nabeel. He pulled out the bangles.

"They are beautiful, *Abbu*!" Mariam exclaimed. "I love the colors. I will wear them for *Eid*!" Then she looked at her father and asked, "Did you get anything for yourself?"

"Yes," he replied, "a pair of pants."

Mariam held up the pants and frowned. "*Abbu*, these are four fingers too long," she said.

"Yes," said Nabeel. "Could you shorten them for me?"

"I'm sorry, *Abbu*. Not today," said Mariam. "I have no time. Tomorrow is *Eid*, and I have to make *samosas* and take care of the baby."

So Nabeel went back home, grabbed a pair of scissors, and cut off a few inches from the bottom of his pants.

Then he hemmed the edges.

"My pants are ready for *Eid*!" he said
and folded them neatly and placed
them on the table.

Then he called to Yasmeen and said
he was going to visit the poor and
sick and give them money for *Eid*.

While Nabeel was out, Yasmeen said to herself, "Nabeel is such a good husband!"

She unfolded his pants, cut off four fingers from the bottom, hemmed the edges, folded them again, and put them back on the table. Then she went into the kitchen to finish her cooking.

While Habiba was making *sheerkorma*, she thought, "Oh, Nabeel is such a good son!"

So she went to Nabeel's house, took his pants, cut off four fingers from the bottom, hemmed the edges, folded them again, and put them back on the table. Then she went back home to finish her cooking.

While Mariam was making *samosas*, she thought, "*Abbu* is such a good father!"

So she went to her father's house, picked up the pants, cut off four fingers from the bottom, hemmed the edges, folded the pants again, and put them back on the table. Then she went back home to finish her cooking.

In the morning, everyone came to Nabeel's house so they could go to the *mosque* together. Yasmeen wore her *burqa*, Habiba wore her bright blue *dupatta,* and Mariam wore her pretty bangles.

"Nabeel!" said Yasmeen. "Try on your pants!"

Just then Habiba came in. "Son!" she said. "Try on your pants!"

Mariam came along, too. "*Abbu*!" she said. "Try on your pants!"

Nabeel looked at them and thought, "They are so wonderful. Even if they didn't have time to shorten my pants, they are still very wonderful!"

He went to his room to put on his pants. His wife and mother and daughter all waited with big smiles on their faces. Suddenly from the bedroom came a howl:

"Ohhhh! Aaaah! Aaaah!"

Ohhh!
Aaaah!
Aaaah!

"What happened?" cried Yasmeen.

"What's the matter?" cried Habiba.

"What's wrong?" cried Mariam.

Nabeel stepped out of his room.

His new *Eid* pants only hung down to his knees!

Yasmeen and Habiba and Mariam all gasped and covered their mouths.

"I cut them by four fingers," said Yasmeen.

"But I cut them by four fingers," said Habiba.

"I cut them by four fingers, too," said Mariam.

"And I cut them by four fingers," said Nabeel.

For a moment there was silence. Then Nabeel began to laugh, and then they all began to laugh!

"Let's sew the pieces back," said Yasmeen.

"Yes, yes, yes!" said Nabeel and watched while Mariam and Habiba and Yasmeen worked on his pants.

In a short while, they were ready and they fit perfectly!

Dressed in their new *Eid* clothes, off they went to the *mosque*!